For the

Mighty, Mighty Halvorsens.

Anton was a young Viking who lived in Norway; a land that was full of rocky places, had cold, shivery winters and endless days in summer that never got dark.

Some Vikings were rather nasty and rough, but Anton came from a good and peaceful clan and even had royal connections. He was adventurous though! Like most Vikings, he longed to explore the world and spent many hours looking toward the horizon wondering what life was like in distant lands. He often watched the big Viking boats as they nudged each other restlessly in the shimmering water.

Summer would be over before long. The family had gathered in the wheat from the fields, picked and preserved berries and stored vegetables for the winter. One evening, Anton's mamma and papa sat down at the table, unrolled a map and laid it out in front of Anton.

'Anton,' said Papa, 'your Uncle Halvar will soon sail to England on urgent Viking business. Would you like to go too and visit your English cousin King Cuthbert? He lives in a castle and is quite important we believe. It will be a long voyage; we will miss you but it will be a big adventure.'

Anton jumped up and down with excitement and couldn't wait to go.

Soon the big day arrived and Uncle Halvar's ship was packed and ready to set sail. As Anton walked towards it with his backpack on his shoulders, he could see nothing but sea all around him and suddenly he felt very small.

He gulped as he waved to his mamma and papa and his cat Scaredy (who was afraid of his own shadow, but bravely came to the water's edge to see him off).

The big Viking ship creaked and groaned as the crew lifted the oars and before long the land was slipping away and his family were just little dots on the shore. Anton felt a bit sad and waved and waved until they were out of sight. He went to his bunk, and the boat swayed a lot as the waves got bigger and bigger as they sailed out to sea. It felt very strange and Anton's tummy felt as though it was flipping upside down for a while, but soon he became used to the feeling and his legs stopped wobbling.

Uncle Halvar spent a lot of time looking out to the horizon and checking their direction. He strode backwards and forwards stroking his beard and said, 'helt fint, helt fint' many times which meant all was good, and Anton felt safe with him at the helm. The journey took a long time and Anton filled his time by helping the crew, until one day, just as the sun was rising, Anton heard uncle Halvar shouting 'land ahoy!'

He looked out and saw a land that was very different from Norway. Here the mountains didn't look as tall as those at home and the grass on the gentle slopes was lush and green.

As he walked down the gangplank and stepped onto the shore, Anton's feet sank into soft golden sand, which stretched off into the distance for miles.

Anton and his uncle walked across the sand towards some rocky steps dug out of the cliff.

Up they climbed until they reached the cliff top. Here Anton saw a very unusual sight. A big house made of stone loomed up in front of him, with a tower that seemed to reach up to the sky.

'This is your cousin Cuthbert's castle,' whispered Uncle Halvar.

Suddenly, there was a loud creaking sound and the door of the castle groaned and squeaked as someone lowered it to the ground. Next, there was a great commotion and some men on horseback blew horns.

A long red carpet was unrolled on the ground and out stepped a very important looking fellow. He was dressed in clothes that seemed to shimmer in the light and there was a cloak around his shoulders edged with fur. On his head was a golden crown studded with gems.

The figure strode over to Anton and thrust his hand out. He went to shake Anton's hand then seemed to think better of it and hugged him tightly instead.

'Welcome, welcome Anton!' He boomed. 'I am your cousin Cuthbert... well... King Cuthbert actually, but don't worry about the King bit, Cuthbert will do. It is simply marvellous to have you here, simply marvellous! You must make yourself right at home.'

Anton listened carefully. He had learned some English words at home but Cuthbert's language sounded very different. He knew he liked Cuthbert very much though and found him to be very friendly.

There was no time for Anton to feel shy in his new surroundings. Cuthbert set off at a fast pace, his cloak billowing behind him. He wanted to show Anton everything! Anton tried to keep up and listen to Cuthbert talking at the same time.

Walking around the grounds, Anton loved the feel of the bouncy grass under his feet and the sound of the sea pounding against the cliffs below.

Soon, the men on horseback trotted off to the castle stables to settle the horses and brush their coats.

'Come Anton,' said Cuthbert, 'I think it's time to show you the castle. Follow me!'

Off they went, Cuthbert whistling merrily as they walked together.

Uncle Halvar bade farewell and promised to return after his important travels. King Cuthbert placed an arm round Anton's shoulders and took him inside.

Inside Cuthbert's castle it was cool and dark. Patterned rugs covered the stone floors and there were strange lifelike figures standing in corners, which were suits of armour.

They climbed up a twisty staircase that wound its way up and up through the castle to the tower. When they reached the top they were a little out of breath! Outside on the stone balcony, Cuthbert showed Anton the view across the whole of his kingdom.

'This is my Kingdom of Crumblyshire, Anton, and it is very important that I look after all the people that live here. They work hard to care for the land and I in turn must care for them.'

Anton thought this sounded like rather a hard job for one man to manage. He noticed that Cuthbert looked tired sometimes and also that Crumbly Castle needed repairs. The roof was leaking and some stone walls had fallen down.

One day when King Cuthbert was busy, engaged in official duties, Anton set out to explore.

Unlike the castle, the land of Crumblyshire was very neat and tidy. Little stone houses sat in the middle of square gardens with fences round them. The trees in the orchards stood in straight rows and their rosy apples looked like someone had polished them that very morning.

The leafy lanes provided shade from the sun and the streams flowed smoothly under the warm stone bridges. All the neighbours were friendly and raised their caps as Anton passed. They spoke of King Cuthbert's kindness and declared Crumblyshire to be the happiest kingdom of all.

As the days passed, Anton learned many things about Crumblyshire and its customs. When Cuthbert had any time off from his kingly duties, he would take Anton to see all the interesting places in his beloved kingdom.

Anton loved exploring the English countryside; the green fields stretched out in front like a patchwork quilt, all he could hear was joyful birdsong and everything was peaceful.

Most of all, Anton liked it when they went to the beach; here Cuthbert would tuck his cloak and crown behind a rock, roll up his trouser legs and go paddling in the sea. Then he didn't seem like a king at all.

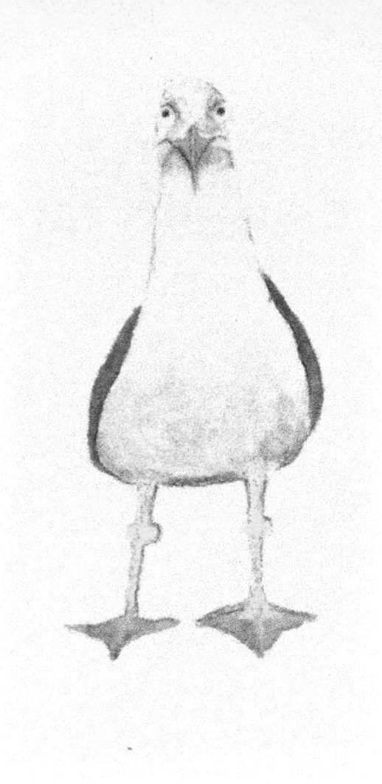

Sometimes when Cuthbert was very busy, Anton stepped in for him. Once, he had the honour of handing out some knighthoods to those people who had performed very brave deeds. The job was very important, and he was careful not to shake as he touched them on each shoulder with Cuthbert's very own sword when they knelt before him.

But no matter what happened each day, when Cuthbert was in residence, at three o'clock in the afternoon, everything, simply everything stopped for tea. Anton and Cuthbert would sit at a table laid out carefully with the King's best china and eat scones with cream and jam and share a pot of tea.

Something worried Anton about his cousin Cuthbert. Each day he watched him ride off on his horse Shadow, to check all was well in Crumblyshire, and sometimes he was away for several days; he was keen to check the land remained peaceful and untroubled by invaders. Meanwhile, Crumbly Castle was, well, crumbling, and the King's own home could not provide him with the shelter he deserved.

Anton hatched a plan. When Cuthbert was away on his travels, he decided he would give Crumbly Castle a makeover. He sent word to the villagers who all came to help. Even Princess Lavender from nearby Luckinghamshire came to lend a hand. She liked King Cuthbert; he often kept an eye on Lucky Castle when she was away.

The team worked for many hours; they repaired the walls and patched up the roof so it was watertight. The local woodcutter chopped many logs and stacked them by the open fireplace so that Cuthbert would keep warm throughout the winter.

They oiled the rusty chain on the drawbridge so whenever there was a hint of trouble, Cuthbert's trusted helpers could raise it in a trice; a good safety measure.

Now the castle and its grounds were as neat and tidy as the rest of Crumblyshire!

King Cuthbert returned to see Anton, Princess Lavender and all his subjects gathered around his beloved castle which gleamed in the sunlight.

He was so happy that he declared the next day to be a public holiday.

Anton's days in England slipped by and soon Uncle Halvar returned to take Anton home to Norway.

As they prepared to leave, it appeared the whole of Crumblyshire had turned out to wave goodbye to Anton. Cuthbert hugged his friend and cousin.

'Thank you for all you have done to help me Anton. I will never forget you. I am not a wealthy King but here is a gift for you to remember me by.'

He handed Anton a velvet pouch of stones collected from the castle grounds. Anton took them carefully; to him they were as valuable as any treasure.

The Viking ship pulled away from the shore to the sound of King Cuthbert's band playing a farewell song, and King Cuthbert waved so hard that his crown nearly fell off.

As he stood on the deck, Anton heard King Cuthbert's voice floating on the breeze... 'Don't forget us dear boy! Cheerio for now.'

When he finally returned home to Norway, Anton told his mamma and papa all about his epic adventure and they listened to his amazing stories.

Later, when Anton unpacked his backpack, he lifted out the velvet pouch of stones. He carefully took them outside the cabin, piled them neatly in the corner of the garden and placed a little English flag on top. Whenever he passed them he thought of his kindly cousin, King Cuthbert of Crumblyshire, England.

The stones remain in Anton's garden to this day... a little piece of England in a foreign land.

Lightning Source UK Ltd.
Milton Keynes UK
UKHW052302300419
341871UK00005B/43/P

Lyn Halvorsen
3, Dimbles Gate, CHINNOR.
OX39 4FP lmhalvo@aol.com

9 781786 235138